TURKEY POX

Laurie Halse Anderson

Illustrated by
Dorothy Donohue

ALBERT WHITMAN & COMPANY • Morton Grove, Illinois

Library of Congress Cataloging-in-Publication Data

Anderson, Laurie Halse.
   Turkey pox / written by Laurie Halse Anderson;
illustrated by Dorothy Donohue.
      p.   cm.
      Summary: Charity has chicken pox, there's a
terrible snowstorm outside, and it looks like the
Chatfields will have to spend Thanksgiving without
Nana and her wonderful roast turkey, stuffing,
and cranberries.
      ISBN 0-8075-8127-5
      [1. Thanksgiving Day—Fiction. 2. Chicken pox—
Fiction. 3. Family life—Fiction. 4. Grandmothers—
Fiction.] I. Donohue, Dorothy, ill. II. Title.
PZ7.A54385Tu   1996   95-52931
[E]—dc20   CIP
                                       AC

Text copyright © 1996 by Laurie Halse Anderson.
Illustrations copyright © 1996 by Dorothy Donohue.
Published in 1996 by Albert Whitman & Company,
6340 Oakton Street, Morton Grove, Illinois
60053-2723.
Published simultaneously in Canada by
General Publishing, Limited, Toronto.
Printed in the United States of America.
10 9 8 7 6 5

Design by Susan B. Cohn.
The text of this book is set in Tekton Bold.
The illustrations are rendered in watercolor and
colored pencil.

The turkey had spots. *Pox.* Nana had dotted its shiny brown skin with cherries stuck on with toothpicks.

Nana kissed the top of Charity's head. "I hear turkey pox is popping up everywhere today."

"Bosh," said Nana. "You don't have chicken pox, you have turkey pox. Look here."

Charity held her breath while her grandmother lifted the lid off the roaster pan.

"OH MY GOODNESS, I DON'T BELIEVE IT," said Aunt Imogene.

Charity scratched her nose. "But
what about my chicken pox?" she asked.
"Don't worry," said one man. "We've all had it."

Nana took off her coat and hat.

"After you called, I looked at that turkey and that turkey looked at me, and just as we started to feel sorry for ourselves, the snowplow caravan came along."

"We plowed all day with no lunch," said the man holding the cranberry sauce.

"I made a deal with the fellows," continued Nana. "If they drove me and the rest of the dinner here, I'd make sure they all enjoyed a hearty meal."

Charity sniffed. Gravy and stuffing. The fourth driver carefully held a glass bowl filled to the top with crimson cranberry sauce.

Four snowplow drivers shuffled in. One man carried a roaster pan steaming with the smell of turkey. Two others held pots.

"It's Nana!" shouted Charity, opening the door. "She came in a snowplow!"

A blast of wind blew her frosty grandmother into the room. Nana hugged Charity, then stuck her head back outside.

"COME AND GET IT, BOYS!" she hollered.

Over the roar they heard a pounding on the front door.
BANG. BANG. BANG.
No one moved.
BANG BANG BANG BANG BANG.
Mom grabbed Dad's arm.
"OPEN UP! I HAVE AN EXPRESS DELIVERY OF HOT TURKEY OUT HERE!"

"ALIENS!" Aunt Imogene screamed. "ALIENS HAVE COME FOR OUR PIES! QUICK, KATHERINE, GET THE GARLIC, GET THE BROOM! PATRICK, DO SOMETHING! I'M GOING TO FAINT!"

Charity stared out the window at the snow-swirling shadows. A flashing orange light was creeping towards the house. Charity rubbed her eyes.

A low rumble started outside, and a second orange light joined the first. More eerie lights whirled and bounced off the living room walls.

The rumble grew to a boom, and the boom to a roar. The windows rattled. Fred turned around.

All because of chicken pox.

Charity peeked at the table. There were mashed potatoes, sweet potatoes, Brussels sprouts with walnuts, apple salad, carrot sticks, celery sticks, and olives. There was a basket of muffins and another of crescent-shaped rolls. The sweet-smelling pies waited on the sideboard: pumpkin, pecan, and mincemeat.

But there was no turkey, no gravy, and no stuffing. Not even a spoonful of cranberry sauce. The best part of dinner was stuck at Nana's house. It would be the first Thanksgiving without Nana. The first Thanksgiving without Nana's turkey.

Mom and Aunt Imogene set out the dinner. "IT'S ALWAYS SOMETHING. IF IT'S NOT ONE THING, IT'S ANOTHER," said Aunt Imogene.

Dad made up a bed on the couch for Charity.
Fred lay right in front of the television so she
couldn't see the parades.

Mom and Dad checked. It was definitely chicken pox. Dad turned the car around. Chicken pox belonged at home.

Mom called Nana on the car phone.

"WHAT DID YOU SAY?" demanded Aunt
Imogene. She looked at Charity.
"SHE *HAS* CHICKEN POX, KATHERINE.
OH MY *GOODNESS!* SHE'S GOT THE POX!
STOP THE CAR!"

The grownups talked about the snowstorm.
It was hard to see the road.
　　Charity itched her knees. Fred made up
a song:

　　　　Charity's neck looks like a giraffe's,
　　　　Charity's covered with spots.
　　　　Charity looks like she took a bath
　　　　in a tub filled with polka dots.

　　Nobody paid attention. Fred sang louder:

　　　　Charity itches her hair and her tummy,
　　　　Charity itches her socks.
　　　　Charity scratches her ears and her ankles.
　　　　I think she's got chicken pox!

After much hustling and bustling, fussing and rushing, packing, stacking, squeezing and squishing, the Chatfields and their holiday meal started their journey. Snow filled the sky.

"PLEASE GET DRESSED, FREDDIE-TEDDIE.
LITTLE BOYS SHOULDN'T EAT THANKSGIVING
DINNER IN THEIR UNDERWEAR!"

Charity itched her knee.

The downstairs clock chimed. The timer dinged. The dryer buzzed. The bathwater gurgled down the drain.

Mom loaded the food into boxes, and Dad buttoned his shirt. Aunt Imogene chased Fred down the hall.

Charity had been ready to go since dawn.
Thanksgiving was her favorite day, and
Nana's roast turkey was her favorite food.
    She watched the upstairs clock tick. She
scratched her stomach.

Aunt Imogene tried to get Cousin Fred to finish his bath. "THE SOAP IS NOT POISON!" she shouted. "DON'T FORGET TO SCRUB YOUR FEET!"

The Chatfields were late for Thanksgiving. Mom stirred the sweet potatoes and sniffed the Brussels sprouts. She had to finish cooking before they left for Nana's.
Dad dumped the laundry into the dryer. He needed a clean shirt.

This book is dedicated
 to the memory of my grandmothers:
Altha (Peg) Holcomb and Anna Evelyn Halse. L.H.A.

For Huz. D.D.